Blue Murder

Beatrix Christian

Currency Press, Sydney,

To Shaar Aerial Christian

CURRENCY PLAYS

First published in 1994
by Currency Press Pty Ltd,
PO Box 2287, Strawberry Hills, NSW, 2012, Australia
enquiries@currency.com.au
www.currency.com.au

Reprinted 2004, 2011, 2018

Cataloguing-in-publication data for this title is available from the National Library
of Australia website: www.nla.gov.au

Typeset by Currency Press.
Cover design by Kate Florance, Currency Press.

Currency Press acknowledges the Traditional Owners of the Country on which we
live and work. We pay our respects to all Aboriginal and Torres Strait Islander
Elders, past and present.

Contents

No generation without corruption

Blue Murder was first performed by Company B at the Belvoir Street Theatre, Sydney on 5th April 1994 with the following cast:

Lucy Bell	EVE
Kelly Butler	ANGEL
Rebecca Frith	LEURA
Sacha Horler	ROSE
Jamie Jackson	LYLE & ROY
Jacek Koman	BLUE

Directed by Antoinette Blaxland
Designed by Dan Potra
Lighting by Rory Dempster
Sound Design by Paul Healy

CHARACTERS

LEURA MACKENZIE, Ghost, first wife, 1880's
ROSE ALLEN, Ghost, second wife, 1930's
ANGEL BROKOWSKY, Ghost, third wife, 1980's
EVELYN CARROL, Fourth wife, contemporary
BLUE, a man
ROY, Official Sweeper
LYLE, a young man

SETTING

The play is set on Blackrock, a natural stone formation, resembling a gothic cathedral, at the centre of Sydney Harbour.

PRODUCTION NOTES

LYLE and ROY to be doubled.
The GHOSTS manifest at the age they were when they were murdered. The GHOSTS have no physical power to influence the material world — they are not poltergeists. They are completely *physically* alienated from the living characters and from each other.
ROY's singing can overlap the dialogue, where necessary.

A NOTE ON PUNCTUATION USED IN THE TEXT

...	= a thought
—	= a hesitation
/	= almost overlapping the end of the previous line
[*pause*]	= an action

ACT ONE

SCENE ONE

Closed train compartment.
EVE *and* LYLE *cheer as the train pulls out of the station.*

EVE: Goodbye, Nowhere. Bye bye sheep. Bye bye moo cows. God I love your cock.

LYLE: I love it that you love it. What are you doing.

EVE: Celebrating. I can't believe we're finally on our way. Quick, undo your jeans before the ticket man gets here.

LYLE: [*unzips his trousers*] You know what I like best about you.

EVE: My bum.

LYLE: You're so romantic.

EVE: Very funny. Romance is for the movies. Wham bam thank you life.

    [*They fuck.*]

LYLE: Happy.

EVE: Yes.

LYLE: Evelyn?

EVE: Yes. Yes, yes.

LYLE: Let's get married. [*Pause.*] Not right away. Once we're settled in Sydney. I've said the wrong thing.

EVE: No.

LYLE: I have.

EVE: Of course not. It's nice of you to ask me.

LYLE: Forget it. Don't stop.

EVE: I can't move, I'm having a panic attack.

LYLE: It was a joke. I was kidding. Besides, you'd be a terrible wife.

EVE: Really?

LYLE: A dead loss.

EVE: Promise?

LYLE: Cross my broken heart.

EVE: Thank you. I never want to get married. I never want to fall in love. Oh Lyle, you know what I mean. [*Fucking him.*] Love. Marriage. Ironing. Death. Worms. Dust. Hyper space.

LYLE: Evelyn /

EVE: My heart's set on getting this job.

LYLE: Evelyn /

EVE: It's incredible that he's even agreed to interview me.

LYLE: Evelyn /

EVE: Think if I actually got it /

LYLE: Shut up, will you. I can hear the conductor.

EVE: Shh. Stop talking.

[*They wait for the conductor to pass and then resume fucking.*]

LYLE: You've always wanted your cake and eat it too.

EVE: I don't like cake. I just want to own the bakery.

LYLE: So can I be your pastry chef.

EVE: You're such a dag.

LYLE: Know what I like least about you.

EVE: What.

LYLE: Your bum.

EVE: Liar.

[*Train into tunnel. Darkness. Sound of waves, loud, louder.*]

SCENE TWO

Blackrock.
Above BLUE*'s desk, a miniature train.* BLUE *writes the next chapter of his own story.*

ROY: [*sings, sweeps*] Morning bird sings,
　　　　　　　　Sun flaps his wings,
　　　　　　　　Birds light the sky,
　　　　　　　　Stars where we lie,
　　　　　　　　Moon in the ground,
　　　　　　　　Make no sound.

> Make a sound,
> Waves wash the shore,
> Sing no more sing no more,
> No more night no more day,
> Sweep away sweep away.
> Sweep away.

BLUE: Bloody sunlight. I'm eclipsed. Heart like a stone. I need a woman.

ROY: Will you go into town then.

BLUE: I'm sick of whores. They should pay me, I'm the one who puts all the effort into it. It's the real thing I want. The Fall. You're only half a man if you separate work and love, Roy. Inspiration and discipline. Woman provides the inspiration and we provide the stick to quiet her /

ROY: I know what you're getting at.

BLUE: Woman. Hard to find one that's just right. How many have I interviewed so far.

ROY: All of them. Only one to go.

BLUE: Never mind.

[*Sings*] Somewhere, someone, just for me.

And then, a walk on the blue moon.

[*Pause.*]

ROY: Here she comes.

EVE: [*enters*] Wow. It's so — Gothic.

ROY: Evelyn Carrol. For the job interview.

BLUE: Spell the name of God.

EVE: G - O - D?

BLUE: Good girl. I like a woman with a sense of humor. A. I. slash E. E. exclamation mark. [*A cry.*] Ai/ee! The Babylonian spelling. My friends call me Blue. You can call me Blue. Your name's obviously Eve, not Evelyn. Eve — Roy.

EVE: Evelyn.

ROY: [*exits*] Official Sweeper.

BLUE: Le Broomier. So. You want to work for me.

EVE: Yes. [*Looking around.*] I think so. I'd love to.

BLUE: And you have no references.

EVE: I edited the school newspaper for three years. I have word processing skills /

BLUE: Word - processing - skills. Do you know my books.

EVE: I'm a fan. [*Long pause.*] I used to have the *A is for Andrew Adam's Appetite* alphabet frieze above my bed. And I love Howard the Hipogriff. He was my best friend when I was a kid. You know how he has a head that tells him to do the right thing and a head that tells him to do the wrong thing /

BLUE: Yes.

EVE: I kind of latched onto that idea.

BLUE: Which one was your favorite?

EVE: *Howard and the Wicked Wand of God.*

BLUE: Which head. [*Pause.*] *The Wicked Wand.* A boy's story.

EVE: I've always been one of the boys. I'm not so interested in girl's stuff.

BLUE: I like that in a woman. Climb trees do you.

EVE: When I was younger.

BLUE: That's the way. Aprons don't flatter anybody.

EVE: No.

BLUE: What's wrong.

EVE: Nothing. [*Pause.*] Deja vu. It sounds silly /

BLUE: Not at all. Metaphysics is my hobby.

    [*Pause.*]

EVE: I don't know much about that. I only just arrived in Sydney this morning.

BLUE: From.

EVE: Nyngan. It was in my resume.

BLUE: Never read them. I make up my mind about a person using gut instinct. The eyes. You've got a woman's eyes. Full of unshed tears.

EVE: I hope not. Well, I edited the school newspaper for three years. I hope to be a writer. [*Pause.*] Eventually.

BLUE: You understand this is a live in position.

EVE: I didn't realize.

BLUE: Are you blushing.

EVE: Am I.

BLUE: It suits you.

EVE: Thank you.

BLUE: There's an initial trial period. The place can feel isolated. I like it. The older I get the fewer people I care to see. Spend too much time with people and you start to feel like you're being trawled through a big ocean in a small net.

EVE: I don't know that many people. Well, no one really interesting.

BLUE: They're only interesting as long as you don't know them. Spring from a large family?

EVE: My dad died last year. It was just the two of us.

BLUE: No mother. Good girl.

EVE: She was really young when I was born. Just passing through.

BLUE: Conceived out of a scuffle in the woods /

EVE: She didn't hang around. Not that I blame her. You know what country towns are like.

BLUE: No. [*Pause.*] Boyfriend?

[*Pause.*]

EVE: No. I'm a free agent.

BLUE: Unusual.

EVE: I suppose so. [*Long pause.*] My dad was the town drunk. Basically, everyone's always expected me to follow in his footsteps. Go off the rails. I was supposed to start sniffing glue or something. You know. Or worse. Something unimaginable. So I made up my mind I wouldn't. No matter what. It's interesting how much people resent it if they offer you a hand out and you don't take it. [*Pause.*] Anyway. They had a cake stall and a raffle for 'Poor Evelyn Carrol' to help pay for the funeral. I donated the cheque to the local AA meeting. And I left. For good. And. Now. Here I am. A free agent.

BLUE: You've lived heroically.

EVE: Thank you.

BLUE: Heroes climb out of their armour after the long, hard battle and then soft white flesh just waiting to be wounded. I like you Eve.

EVE: It's Evelyn.

BLUE: Let's see if you can keep up with me.

EVE: There are some things I'd like to ask you about the job /

BLUE: How old was your mother when you were born.

EVE: Fifteen.

BLUE: Fifteen. A country town. Unwanted teenage pregnancy. Never mind. Ready?

EVE: I only did shorthand for one semester /

BLUE: A dark wood. A silver pond. The pond, like a magic paper weight, shows under its crust of clear ice the story of sperm and egg, temporarily frozen and immaculate. Now. Eve's unlucky, unmarried mother sees what the pond shows her and bursts into childish tears of remorse.

EVE: Actually, they were married. [*Pause.*] Sort of /

BLUE: Just unlucky then. She discovers a steaming trail of blood red spoors which melt the ice like acid. She follows this trail into a dark grove. The Devil stands in the shadows, scratching himself, waiting for her to follow the residue of his scarlet eczema. The Devil hates the spooky woods and wants to hightail it back into Sydney as soon as possible. 'Hello Little Mother,' the Devil says. 'Need a favour? Anything I can help you with?' [*Pause.*] Are you with me.

EVE: It's not exactly a documentary is it.

BLUE: Eve's nervous mum replies, 'Can you take the child from my womb?'

EVE: My mother would never have had an abortion.

BLUE: Obviously. A bit of chat ensues. 'Moral dilemma', blah blah blah. Then the Devil positions Eva's Madre at the centre of the grove and begins to dance. 'Ai/ee! is my lord! Ai/ee! is my god! Ai/ee! is a mountain! Ai/ee! is my helper! Ai/ee! is surpassing! Ai/ee! is a warrior! She of Ai/ee! Mercy Oh Ai/ee! I have proved true Oh Ai/ee!' 'Ai/eee! went forth! Ai/eee! is a wall! Name of Ai/eeee! Ai/eee! stays in good health! Ai/eee! is my mother! Ai/eee! is a harp!' With that, Dev. collects his sealskin coat which has been tossed over a tree stump. 'When do I lose the child?' asks the pregnant girl, by now frightened and confused. 'When she draws her first breath,' he says. And Eve's mum is horrified to see his heavy gold loin cloth lifted by a sudden erection. [*Pause.*] Well?

EVE: Well ... Nyngan's a hole, basically. End of the train line.

BLUE: As my assistant I'd expect you to bring something to the work.
    [*Pause.*]

EVE: Sealskin coat could be changed. [*Pause.*] It's environmentally unsound ...

BLUE: It's Lucifer's coat.

EVE: Right. That makes sense.

BLUE: Perhaps the devil should be a woman. Lucifer *is* a fallen angel. What man could fall so far from grace as an ugly woman.

EVE: Are you serious.

BLUE: Obviously you believe the Devil's a man.

EVE: No. I don't have an opinion one way or the other. I don't believe in the devil. I mean, I'm not religious. Are you.

BLUE: No. What *do* you believe?

EVE: Well, I believe people — we — are responsible for the world we live in. Here. Now. Ourselves.

BLUE: Very American of you. I suppose you believe in free will as well.

EVE: Free will. [*Pause.*] Yes. Yes I do.

BLUE: I never hit it off with French philosophers. Pussy whipped by their mothers. History is a tidal wave of blood and free will is the little white flag we wave at it before it breaks. Again.
    [*Pause.*]

EVE: I realize I still have a lot to learn.

BLUE: Good girl.

EVE: That's one of the reasons I'd love to work for you.

BLUE: Call me Blue.

EVE: Blue. If you give me a chance you won't regret it /

BLUE: You intrigue me.

EVE: Me?

BLUE: So lovely.

EVE: Thank you.

BLUE: So smart.

EVE: Thank you.

BLUE: So alone. And destiny's a balloon with a very short string. Better grab it while we can.

SCENE THREE

Blackrock.

EVE: Meet Evelyn Carrol. Personal assistant extraordinaire.

LYLE: I knew you'd get it.

EVE: Shh! You'll have to leave, I start right away. Sorry. He's really eccentric. He'd be furious if he saw you out here. [*Pause.*] He's a recluse.

LYLE: Only you could get a job within hours of arriving in town. Tell me everything. Start at the beginning.

EVE: Lylo ...

LYLE: What. [*Pause.*] What.

EVE: It's a live in position but I'm sure I'll have heaps of time off.

LYLE: Live in?

EVE: Writers don't work 9 to 5 you know.

LYLE: What, so you have to stay. Now. For the rest of the week.

EVE: Yes.

LYLE: We just got here. What about finding a flat.

EVE: You'll have to do it.

LYLE: I'm sure if you explain /

EVE: I've agreed.

LYLE: Can't you at least start tomorrow.

EVE: We've started. I can't hang around here either.

LYLE: Oh — excuse me. [*Pause.*] Something's wrong here /

EVE: It's amazing. I'm doing creative work already. A story ... for teenagers, about ... issues.

LYLE: Live in.

EVE: I know.

LYLE: Why. Do you have to do the housework or something /

EVE: No! It's nothing like that. Besides, there's Roy. He's like ... a butler.

LYLE: A butler. Well then.

EVE: We'll go sight seeing on the weekend. Please, please, please. Don't be cross. Be happy for me.

LYLE: I am. I'm happy for you. What choice have I got.

EVE: None. [*Pause.*] I know I'm impossible.

LYLE: When do I get to meet him.

EVE: Eventually. It's not as if I had a chance to discuss my private life or anything.

    [*Silence.*]

LYLE: Well. Congratulations. It's wonderful. Really. I'm proud of you.

    [*Pause.*]

EVE: Don't go yet. Now I'm starting to feel nervous.

LYLE: Nah. You're my tough little nut. It's the thing I really like best about you. Give me the number. I'll call you this afternoon.

EVE: No phone. He's a very private person. A real old eccentric. Trust me. I'd better go back in. I'll call you as soon as I can. Go. Go.

LYLE: When.

EVE: I'm not sure yet — about my actual hours ...

LYLE: Can't you just ask.

EVE: Please.

LYLE: [*vampire voice*] If I don't hear from you I'll meet you here at midnight. Friday. When the moon is full.

    [*Pause.*]

EVE: Good idea.

LYLE: Evelyn?

EVE: What.

LYLE: Don't think I love you or anything.

EVE: I won't.

ACT TWO

SCENE ONE

Blackrock.
BLUE *writes the next chapter of his own story.*

ROY: [*sings, sweeps*] Sweet woman sings,
                Crow flaps his wings,
                Cloud in the sky,
                Sweet woman cries,
                Tears on the ground —
BLUE: Can't hear myself think.
ROY: [*sings*]   Moon homeward bound,
                Waves wash the shore,
                Sing no more /
BLUE: For Heaven's sake Roy it's clean as a whistle in here.
ROY: [*sings*]   Say no more /
BLUE: Sweep away. Every last shred of inspiration. Public servant.
ROY: [*sings*]   Sing no more. Finished.
     Official Sweeper. That's my job. [*Exits.*] Yellow sun's down.
EVE: What exactly does Roy do.
BLUE: Sweeps. I hate Howard. I hate children.
EVE: Why do you write kid's books then.
BLUE: Political reasons. Get to them young.
       [*He hands manuscript of 'Howard Goes Shopping' to* EVE.]
BLUE: Children are small, mean, unimaginative versions of which-
     ever parent is least appealing.
EVE: [*reads*] 'Howard's trick worked. The security guard thought
     the naughty hipogriff was a stuffed toy. Hoorah! At last! Howard
     is alone in the department store after closing time.' I like it.
BLUE: We don't need 'after closing time'.

[EVE *crosses it out.*]

BLUE: God I loathe my job. Work's the opiate of the masses.

EVE: *Howard Goes Shopping* will be a best seller.

BLUE: It's not firing.

EVE: Can I suggest something.

BLUE: Please do.

EVE: Howard has two heads. He could go to the hat department and try on hats.

    [*Pause.*]

BLUE: Not bad. Off you go then.

EVE: Me? Right. [*Pause.*] Um. 'Howard went to the escalators. [*Pause.*] He rode down the ... "down" escalator to the hat department. He found a hat for his happy head and a hat for his sad head.'

BLUE: 'One of the display dummies wore a trench coat, a toy gun and a cigar. Howard put on the coat. He put the gun in his pocket. Then the naughty hipogriff lit the yummy cigar.'

EVE: Ha ha.

BLUE: 'The terrible cigar made him cough and feel dizzy.' No. Sneeze. 'Sneeze and feel dizzy. Sick ...'

EVE: Dizzy.

BLUE: 'Dizzy. He threw it away. Horror! The cigar has started a little fire. Meanwhile. In the bargain basement. A robber has sneaked in. Dangerous robber' /

EVE: Hang on. I know, I know. It's Fritz and Fritz.

BLUE: Fritz and Fritz. Yes. They were in something else /

EVE: *Howard Saves Father Christmas*. It'll be really good because he's had a run in with them before /

BLUE: so we don't have to do more drawings, they're already on file. Good girl.

EVE: When they see him they say, 'Oh no, it's Howard!'

BLUE: Yes. That'll do for today. You know Evie /

EVE: Evelyn. Evelyn.

BLUE: Howard began life as a hipogriff with dignity. A true existential anti hero. One head for watching his step, one for watching his back. No one liked him, he didn't give a damn.

EVE: That's why children relate to him. He's got no friends, he's lonely. Like them.

BLUE: I don't care if they relate to him or not. Little wimps /

EVE: Well, I like this story. I'd love to have the run of a department store overnight.

BLUE: Because you're simple.

EVE: I beg your pardon.

BLUE: Blinded by matter. Deafened by it. It's too late for you. But Howard's going to free children from the tyranny of toys. He'll burn that department store to the ground.

EVE: I resent being called simple.

BLUE: Matter grates on the imagination /

EVE: I said I resent being called simple.

BLUE: Let me tell you what your life has been. Dust. You haven't drawn a single breath yet.

EVE: You couldn't know what my life has been.

BLUE: Sweep away. What you think, what you believe. Your plans. Your expectations. Drop the lot into the ocean like a sack of rats. Have you got what it takes to start a new life.

EVE: That's why I left home.

BLUE: Then liberate yourself.

EVE: I am.

[BLUE *laughs.*]

When I stepped onto that train to come to Sydney it was an amazing moment for me /

BLUE: That train didn't exist.

EVE: Oh really? The fact is, it got me *here*.

BLUE: Fate, not fact. It's time to move on.

[*Pause.*]

EVE: Is the trial period over.

BLUE: Time to say goodbye. To 'Evelyn Carrol'. Fate is a tuning fork. One pure note. Listen for it. And when you hear it, strive to hit it. Ignore everything else. What do you hear.

EVE: The sea. And you.

SCENE TWO

Blackrock.

BLUE *writes the next chapter of his own story.*

ROY: [*enters, sings*] Old night owl sings,

                    Sun unfolds his wings,

                    Bats sweep the sky,

                    I bid you good bye.

BLUE: Tell me about your very first romance.

ROY: [*sings*]   Put the dead in the ground,

                    Make no sound.

                    Make a sound.

BLUE: Thank you Roy.

EVE: Thought I was supposed to forget the past.

BLUE: I don't mean it literally. Literalism's a disease /

EVE: Whatever.

ROY: [*sings*]   The dead have their say /

                    Sweep away sweep away /

BLUE: Thank you Roy.

ROY: Sickle Tide. [*Exits.*] Red sun's in its season.

EVE: Anyway, I don't believe in romance.

BLUE: Most women don't, it's a mug's game. Your first fuck then.

EVE: How do you know I'm not a virgin. [*Pause.*] You want me to make something up.

BLUE: What. In the age of realism.

EVE: Ha ha. [*Pause.*] I bonked the local minister.

BLUE: Good girl. Eve, adrift, on a vast blue altar cloth, like a pre-Raphaelite virgin. Too flowery?

EVE: Just a bit.

BLUE: Did you hope for a miraculous escape. Of course, who wouldn't. You cross yourself. No point merely hoping when you could be praying.

EVE: Blue /

BLUE: The priest locks up his church. Loud click. Slow wink. 'Holy Augusta, I've missed my chance to escape.' Eve thinks. Prematurely. And then she misses her chance again. And then, again.

EVE: No prayers necessary. I wasn't trying to escape.

BLUE: Later. Same day. Eve, exhausted. How her poor throat aches.

EVE: Yuck.

BLUE: From calling out god's name. The *unromantic* church has the overall appearance of a high ranking S.S. officer's office. Eve is now the mesmerized victim of a humming refrigeration unit and the chilly atmosphere.

EVE: It wasn't in the church /

BLUE: 'I know you didn't have an orgasm,' the priest says. 'Do you know what an orgasm is?' You cover your heart with your hands and back away. Straight into a statue of the Virgin. The Virgin crashes to the floor and explodes into a thousand pieces. [*Remembering.*] Splinters of plaster fly in all directions, stained glass rains down like a storm of passionate blood.

EVE: It was nothing /

BLUE: He suddenly senses, as we all do, that every woman might be our last.

EVE: Look. It wasn't like that. He wasn't a priest, he was a fruit cake. The day I 'lost my virginity', I don't know. It was just another day. Except the whole town decided to let him 'baptize' me in the river. Baaa. Like sheep. Down to the river. He pushed my head under water. The water was yellow. The river had just about dried up by then. People shouted, 'Saved.'

BLUE: Saved.

EVE: I took him off behind the pub.

BLUE: Upon the stony ground.

EVE: Beer garden. Dad was inside drinking. [*Pause.*] What we did lasted about a minute. Basically I felt cold and wet. Okay? Not worth remembering.

BLUE: You've never forgotten it.

EVE: It didn't mean anything.

BLUE: And.

EVE: And nothing. [*Long pause.*] And I was really angry at my mother. For abandoning me.

BLUE: The humpy blues.

EVE: Stupid.

BLUE: I like your story.

EVE: It's not a 'story'. It's my life.

BLUE: You felt alone. You've always felt alone. [*Pause.*] You've grown up among barbarians in the new dark ages, you have to find your own kind.

EVE: They were Methodists /

BLUE: You left as soon as you could.

EVE: There was no work /

BLUE: You dreamed of something more, something finer.

EVE: Everyone does /

BLUE: Stop fighting me. You woke up one day and looked at everything that was most familiar and you wanted to scream because it disgusted you. And you ran away in horror.
[*Pause.*]

EVE: Yes. Only I don't see it as running away.

BLUE: You're so young.

EVE: I'm not a child.

BLUE: You're angry.

EVE: You say 'literalism's a disease'. I'm not stupid. I know what you mean. I'm boring. Basically you're saying I have no imagination.

BLUE: No. You're frightened, that's all. Still running.

EVE: From what?

BLUE: The truth of who you are. But a life that doesn't grow out of that truth will merely come to an end as it began. Still-born.

EVE: I understand that. You want something. You want me to be something ...

BLUE: If your imagination doesn't ravish you you'll have a predictable life. Dust.

EVE: Why do you care. What difference does it make to you.

BLUE: Without that you're no good to me. [*Pause.*] I'm writing a story. I've been working on it for a long time. I find myself unable to finish it.

EVE: A 'Howard' book?

BLUE: No. This story is my truth.

EVE: And you think I can help you finish it?

BLUE: Yes.

EVE: What if I can't /

BLUE: Here we are.

SCENE THREE

Blackrock.

ROY: [*enters, sings*] Moon in the sky,
Woman must die,
The dead have their say,
Sweep away sweep away,
Waves wash the shore,
Sing no more say no more.
Sing no more.

[*Exits.*]

Moonlight.

BLUE: Eve, so beautiful, so fair. Seaweed in her hair. Heaven sent, from blue to Blue.

EVE: Put me down. I hate having my feet off the ground.

[*He spanks her, still holding her and spinning.*]

Don't! Don't do that!

BLUE: [*holds out his hand*] Why does it behave so badly.

EVE: Because it's *your* hand I suppose.

BLUE: Repulsive. Never mind. No lifeline. Destiny cut short. Heart line wiped out. My wife came at me with a knife, I grabbed the blade, we struggled. Politics and love. Oil and water.

EVE: What happened.

BLUE: It ended.

[*Pause.*]

EVE: Poor hand.

[*She kisses his hand.* BLUE *still holds her.*]

I didn't realize you were married /

BLUE: You plant an acorn. What will it become.

EVE: I'm sick of stories.

BLUE: Play with me.

[*Pause.*]

EVE: An oak tree.

16

BLUE: Wrong. Try again.

EVE: Acorn, oak tree.

BLUE: Use your imagination.

EVE: I can't think what else it could be /

BLUE: [*quiet*] Gypsies dance in the acorn field. An alchemist emp-
ties her pail of chemicals into it. The Devil marches through it in
bloody boots. The poor, frightened, little acorn absorbs everything. She evolves, she transmogrifies, into a slippery hipogriff
with its tail rooted so deeply in the dirt some hungry Chinaman
will mistake it for a radish.

EVE: Then why have I seen hundreds of oak trees and not a single
hipogriff.

BLUE: Because your beautiful eyes are for staring into, not for seeing out of. Let yourself bask in my gaze. If you keep perfectly
still during sex, if you don't move a muscle for an hour, or longer,
one sudden, sharp intake of breath will reverse the direction of
your blood. A superior pleasure, as well as being extremely good
for the digestion. [*Pause.*] Paradise has many gardens. [*Pause.*]
Evelyn.

[*Pause.*]

EVE: My name's — Eve.

BLUE: When you look at me like this Eve, I feel as if I'm the one
being seduced.

EVE: You've got such a red mouth.

BLUE: Don't look away.

EVE: Do you want to kiss me.

BLUE: Would you run.

EVE: I want to kiss you.

BLUE: Are you frightened.

EVE: No.

BLUE: Slowly then. Slowly. As radiant as the very first woman. Each
limb a garden. Blackrock has many gardens, all of them right
here in this bed.

EVE: Blue.

BLUE: Nice underwear. That's important.

EVE: Kiss me.

BLUE: Shh. Shh. Abandon yourself.

[*The Walls murmur.* EVE *doesn't hear.*]

EVE: I am.

BLUE: Fall. Let yourself fall.

EVE: I'm trying.

BLUE: The relief is unimaginable.

EVE: I hope so.

BLUE: Forsake yourself.

EVE: Yes.

[*At the same time, the Walls whisper, 'No'.*]

BLUE: Hold nothing back. Abandon yourself.

EVE: Yes.

[*At the same time, the Walls whisper, 'No'.*]

BLUE: Eve.

EVE: Kiss me.

BLUE: Gain the world, lose nothing.

EVE: Please.

BLUE: Say only yes.

EVE: Yes. Yes.

BLUE: Yes to life.

EVE: Yes.

BLUE: Yes to the future.

EVE: Yes.

BLUE: No fruit is forbidden. Taste all of life.

EVE: I want to. I will. Kiss me.

[*They begin to fuck. The Walls are full of voices. Suddenly, the ghosts of* LEURA, ROSE, *and* ANGEL *appear.* LEURA, *1880's.* ROSE, *1930's.* ANGEL, *1980's.* EVE *can't hear or see the* GHOSTS.]

ANGEL: What are you doing.

ROSE: The fiery church, a great black oven inside and all the un-leavened brides.

ANGEL: You prick. Get off of her.

EVE: Yes.

ANGEL: No.

BLUE: Not yet.

ROSE: All the tiny white sparrow brides, veils flying out behind. Mouth pursed into O's of horror.

LEURA: Shut up Rose.
EVE: [*together with* ANGEL] Yes.
ANGEL: [*together with* EVE] No!
BLUE: No /
EVE: It's alright.
BLUE: Not yet.
LEURA: Can she see anything.
ANGEL: Blue, look at me. Look at me.
LEURA: Can she hear us. Can she see us.
BLUE: Oh god.

    [*Orgasm. Fog horn. Silence. The* GHOSTS *disappear.*]
ANGEL: Cunt!
LEURA: Another poor blind thing.
ROSE: Lasciatemi morir!

ACT THREE

SCENE ONE

Blackrock.

EVE *writes, she can't concentrate.* EVE *finally gives up and explores. As* EVE *explores, she releases* BLUE*'s memories.* ROY *follows her into a part of Blackrock that's been closed for a long time. He sweeps.*

ROY: Here you are.
    [*Pause.*]
EVE: Roy, how long have you worked for Blue.
ROY: I don't work for anyone. I belong to Blackrock.
EVE: Right.
ROY: I'm official.
EVE: Of course.
ROY: He lives here. I live here.
EVE Right. [*Pause.*] It's an amazing place.
ROY: Rises out of the water and falls, in and out, in and out and us riding on its back.
EVE: Yes.
ROY: Blackrock has stone roots that go right under the harbour, even underneath Sydney. Cathedral Rock, once. Then they built St. Mary's and the City Council changed our name.
EVE: Really.
ROY: Yep.
EVE: You don't really clean anything, do you Roy. [*Pause.*] I mean, you broom's not doing much for the rug.
ROY: I sweep. My father was old fashioned, he believed one broom was enough. But I've got wide brooms, narrow, hard and scratchy, soft as silk, horsehair, bright pink nylon. Mixed bristle.
EVE: That's a lot of brooms.
ROY: Straw, of course.

EVE: Of course. I like the feel of a room after you've swept. It feels calm. Spacious.

ROY: I've been called a Zen sweeper in my day.

EVE: I can imagine. A Zen sweeper ...

ROY: If you sweep away strong feeling and worldly desires you can find peace.

EVE: Don't you ever — get sick of it.

ROY: It's my job.

[*Pause.* EVE *opens a door.*]

The studio.

EVE: Right ...

[*A covered easel.* EVE *picks up* LEURA*'s sketch book and leafs through it.* LEURA *frees herself from the Wall during the scene.* BLUE *appears.*]

LEURA: I like this costume.

BLUE: Keep still.

LEURA: I'll not be taking it off.

BLUE: I'm painting a series of historical figures, not nudes.

LEURA: So you said. But people are susceptible to lying, particularly in advertisements.

BLUE: A cynic. Good girl.

LEURA: Cynicism is a style of exaggeration. I favour the truth.

BLUE: Then you must diaspprove of my work.

LEURA: You're an artist. And a man. You needn't solicit my approval.

BLUE: As an artist and a man I'm obliged to solicit the approval of women or fall into despair.

LEURA: In that case. I think your paintings are very finely executed.

BLUE: Don't flatter me.

LEURA: In that case. I mistrust Romanticism as a style.

BLUE: Keep still. Your hair speaks to me. History. Desire.

LEURA: I'll cut it off and sell it to you if you like.

BLUE: Thank you. You possess a charming sharp tongue as well.

[*Silence.*]

LEURA: I'll paint you in a fortress of light, and make you inviolable. Belphoebe, the Warrior Queen. Looking out into the future, where all women are free.

LEURA: Artists can afford to be idealists.

BLUE: Merely another burden.

LEURA: Hardly a burden when you can choose when to pick it up and when to put it down.

BLUE: Perhaps you want to leave. [*Pause.*] How stubborn you are. Your heritage no doubt. Your parents, are they /

LEURA: Dead.

BLUE: Ah. Not from Scotland as I'd supposed. And you impoverished.

LEURA: I have my hair.

BLUE: A sad story. But circumstance has created an admirable woman. If you stay, you'll have to match me in my pursuit of a truth, which instinct tells me, you have so far denied yourself.

LEURA: Which truth is that.

BLUE: The pursuit of Beauty.

LEURA: A freedom so far denied me. And all my sex.

BLUE: That's why your eyes are clear as morning and mine dim as the passing day.

LEURA: Don't flatter *me*.

BLUE: Stay. Shame me into a frenzy of art.

LEURA: Instinct tells me you're a stranger to shame. But I need employment.

EVE: [*reads*] Leura. Leura Mackenzie /

LEURA: [*emerges fully*] And I would like to be Belphoebe.

[EVE *moves to uncover the easel.* ROY *sweeps her out of the room.*]

SCENE TWO

EVE: I've never seen the curtains open.

ROY: He prefers a private view.

EVE: And the lights are always on.

ROY: The night here is very dark. He prefers his own light.

EVE: There isn't one clock here.

ROY: There's the rhythm of the waves. Washes everything away.

EVE: I wake up, dreaming, but I can't remember the dream.

ROY: People who live here forget. Memory goes. That's the sea.

EVE: Yes. Yes.

[EVE *opens a door.*]

ROY: The library.

[EVE *picks up* ROSE*'s notebooks. Reads them.* ROSE *frees herself from the Wall during this scene.* BLUE *and* LEURA *appear.*]

BLUE: I can't wait to hear your poems.

ROSE: I've never shown them before. They're just scribble /

BLUE: Did anyone see you leave.

ROSE: No /

BLUE: What an adventure /

ROSE: Yes.

LEURA: Run Rosie run.

BLUE: Don't be frightened.

ROSE: Oh I'm always frightened. [*Pause.*] Are you writing something new. Something wonderful.

BLUE: A poem about you.

ROSE: I wrote about you too.

BLUE: It's not finished yet. Come on then. I'll read them out if you'd rather.

ROSE: No, no my handwriting's impossible. Promise not to laugh. Oh. How embarrassing.

BLUE: You've gone bright red. I'll have to call you Rose.

ROSE: No. Not that one. Oh no. That bit's dire.

BLUE: Where's the one about me.

ROSE: I couldn't.

BLUE: Sweet Rosamund prithee get on with it lest boredom straddle me with her leaden thighs.

ROSE: Sorry. It's a prose-poem-thing. Don't you just adore French poetry.

BLUE: Whose.

ROSE: Baudelaire. He's my hero.

BLUE: We're related by blood. I'm surprised you've read that particular poet.

ROSE: The nuns have a big library, they read and read till their eyes drop out.

BLUE: I'm shocked.

ROSE: Oh, not that poet of course, he's Sister Anne's. She reads European literature so she'll have something to confess. She's hugely fat with at least six bosoms.

BLUE: And she lends you books so she can watch you sin, in her room in the dead of night, by the light of a candle.

ROSE: Gosh no. I have to steal them. I know her hidey place. And I don't always put them back, but she can't exactly ask me for them, can she.

BLUE: Perhaps she doesn't want to.

ROSE: That's nothing. The things I could tell.

BLUE: I can hardly wait.

LEURA: [*overlapping*] I can hardly wait.

ROSE: It's not a traditional poem, in the old fashioned sense, it's a Dialogue. Me speaking to my mother. Who's dead. Not in the Dialogue. In real life. I often write to her. Sometimes — it sounds cracked — but sometimes I write back to myself. From her. As if she were alive. Are you sure you want to hear this. Alright. Ready?

BLUE: As a Stilton cheese.

ROSE: [*reads*] 'Girl'. That's me. 'I've met a man! His name is Blue! He's asked to marry me!'

BLUE: [*laughs*] No. Go on. Go on. I will have to ask you, I'm sure.

ROSE: I told you it was dire.

BLUE: Rose. Forgive me.

ROSE: No.

BLUE: I'm a moron. I've made you suffer.

ROSE: I was suffering before I met you thank you very much.

BLUE: Then I can't make you suffer, if you suffer already. How modern of you.

EVE: [*reads*] Rosemary Allen /

ROSE: [*emerges fully*] I'll just have to make you suffer instead.
　　　　[ROY *puts back the notebook. He sweeps* EVE *out of the room.*]

SCENE THREE

EVE: How often has Blue been married.

ROY: Three times.

[*Pause.*]

EVE: What were they like.

ROY: Angel was a stripper.

EVE: God.

ROY: Broke his heart, sneaked off in the night.

EVE: I suppose she was really exotic.

ROY: No.

EVE: What about — Rosemary.

[*Pause.*]

ROY: Marriage isn't a way of life for some women.

EVE: What do you mean. [*Pause.*] I suppose you made friends with them.

ROY: I liked Rose and she liked me.

EVE: Saying goodbye must've been sad.

ROY: She just went. We didn't say goodbye.

EVE: Was Rosemary the one who hacked up Blue's hand /

ROY: No! That was Leura. Leura locked up my brooms. I told her to get on one and fly away.

EVE: Roy! So, how many times has Blue been /

ROY: You should try sweeping.

[EVE *accepts the broom.*]

[*Counts time*] Sweep ... sweep ...

LEURA: This world is a better world for being so often swept.

ROY: ... not like that /

EVE: How long have you been here, Roy.

ROY: My father was here. His father was here. You don't have to do anything. You're not the broom.

EVE: You must know Blue pretty well /

ROY: He likes to churn things up. I sweep. I breath in. Tides ebb. There's flowing. All our lives, yours, mine, all the the people in the whole of Sydney put together are just the foam in a single wave. Hopeless. [*Taking broom.*] Do I look like a broom. A broom is a broom. Is a broom.

[EVE *opens a door. Pause.*]

Blue's room.

[EVE *looks at* ANGEL*'s and* BLUE*'s personal things* — *toiletries,*

25

clothes. ANGEL *frees herself from the Wall during this scene.*
BLUE, LEURA *and* ROSE *appear.*]

BLUE: Angel.

ANGEL: Surprise!

BLUE: What closed door is not an invitation to her.

ANGEL: You must be wondering why I'm here. [*Pause.*] I probably shouldn't have come. Spur of the moment thing. [*Long pause.*] You haven't been in to watch the show the last few weeks. [*Long pause.*] I've missed you. [*Long pause.*] I should leave.

BLUE: Always sneaking never snuck.

ANGEL: What.

BLUE: No. How.

ANGEL: What.

BLUE: How. Your harbour taxi's gone. By what means do you intend leaving.

ANGEL: I don't know. I hadn't thought about it. How do *you* get off the rock. [*Pause.*] I'm really fucked if I know actually. I wasn't thinking about leaving when I came over. I thought you might be pleased to see me. Obviously, I made a mistake. Typical really. Fucking typical.

LEURA: Fucking typical.

ROSE: Leura!

BLUE: Angel ...

ANGEL: Let me guess. You're married. To Roy. Just kidding. Why have you stopped coming to see the show.

BLUE: Because I finally understood something, watching you dance. You take off one G-string, then another, then another. But there's always one more to go. A woman is what can never be reached. Even naked, she withholds her final secret.

ANGEL: I don't get it. I invited you home — you said no.

BLUE: I'm not speaking anatomically. [*Pause.*] I can't embark on another love affair.

ANGEL: You said you felt drawn to me /

BLUE: If I make a commitment to my feelings for you, a horrible actuality encroaches as potentiality drains away. If I abandon you, potentiality is regained as actuality fades. Either way I lose. Love or the beloved /

ANGEL: Hang on. You're worried about how it's going to end before you even do it. That's stupid. You know why I came out here. Because I wanted to see you. Simple. I like you. A lot. I think about you all the time. I want to be with you. [*Pause.*] I wear my heart on my sleeve. That's the way I am. Some people don't like that.

LEURA: I wear my heart on my sleeve /

ROSE: Don't Leura /

BLUE: I like it. Even down on all fours on that stage Angel, you're the Queen of Heaven.

ANGEL: You're gorgeous, you know that. I'm here now. Might as well stay. For a while. [*Pause.*] Are you busy.

BLUE: Avoiding 'Howard the Hipogriff'.

ANGEL: Yeah? Have you got any kids /

BLUE: Children are monstrous.

ANGEL: You wouldn't feel that way about your own.

BLUE: Vampires.

ANGEL: I plan on having at least five /

BLUE: Succubi.

ANGEL: maybe eight. [*Pause.*] Call me extravagant.

BLUE: You're extravagant.

ANGEL: Why do you write kid's books then, if /

BLUE: It's a calling. I'm a mediocre painter and a bad poet. But I've made a fortune writing children's books. Strange, how life turns out.

ANGEL: It sure is. I've never known a writer before. I knew a film maker once.

EVE: [*reads*] Angel. Angel ... Brokowski /

ANGEL: [*emerges fully*] Listen, do you want to fuck me?

BLUE: Yes.

ANGEL: Good. Great.

BLUE: But not today.

ANGEL: What's the problem.

BLUE: No problem. A miser enjoys his money all the more for never spending it.

ANGEL: You're no miser.

SCENE FOUR

Blackrock.

All converge on BLUE. LEURA *fixes on* ROY. ANGEL *fixes on* BLUE.

ANGEL: Are you two writing a love story.

LEURA: This world is a better world for being so often swept.

EVE: Good morning.

ANGEL: Are you.

BLUE: Good morning.

LEURA: The broom is the breath of the sweeper.

EVE: Everything alright.

LEURA: [*to* ROY] Monster.

BLUE: Fine.

EVE: Good.

LEURA: Monster.

EVE: Sleep alright.

BLUE: Fine.

EVE: Good. I've had a great idea for a new story.

ANGEL: You promised the one we wrote would be your last.

EVE: At least — I think it's a great idea.

ANGEL: Are you. Or not /

LEURA: Leave it.

EVE: Is anything wrong.

ANGEL: Yes. Or no.

BLUE: Migraine.

LEURA: Leave it!

EVE: Can I do anything?

ANGEL: Yes. Or. No.

BLUE: [*to* ANGEL] Be quiet.

EVE: Sorry.

LEURA: Let the past pile up, put the bodies out in the sun till the whole of Sydney's drunk on the fumes.

ANGEL: Blue.

LEURA: A century. One hundred years.

ANGEL: Simple. Simple. Yes. Or no.

LEURA: Watching. Watching. I stay awake. I stay awake.

ROSE: Lasciatemi morir.

ANGEL: You are.

LEURA: And for what.

ANGEL: A fucking love story.

ROSE: Lasciatemi morir.

LEURA: Justice for all. No justice for women.

ANGEL: Are you going to marry her.

LEURA: The devil is a broom.

ANGEL: Blue.

LEURA: [*to* ANGEL] It's over.

ROSE: Stop it Leura. It's her first time /

LEURA: He has finished with you.

ANGEL: Get away from me. Blue /

LEURA: He can't even bring himself to look at you now /

ROSE: Leura /

ANGEL: Get away. Blue. Look at me.

EVE: Are you alright.

ANGEL: What's going on.

BLUE: [*at* ANGEL] I am not accountable to you.

EVE: Sorry /

BLUE: I'll do as I please in my own house.

EVE: Of course /

BLUE: Women!

ACT FOUR

SCENE ONE

Courtyard. The Nowhere Stairs — a flight of stairs that leads to nowhere.
Foghorn. ROSE *enters.* ROSE *rushes up the Nowhere Stairs to watch a ship leave the harbour. She waves at it.* ANGEL *enters.*

ANGEL: Blue's sick. Boring as.

ROSE: I love it when they go off. Come up Angel. She's a beauty. If I'd been a boy I would have run away to sea /

ANGEL: When I met Blue he promised to take me to Buenos Aries. It's got the classiest shops in the world. That's where I wanted to go for our honeymoon. I said, 'Blue, I want to go shopping in Buenos Aries.'

    [LEURA *enters.*]

He said, 'Baby, the whole wide world's right here between your legs.' God he's filthy.

LEURA: Angel ...

ANGEL: Don't start.

ROSE: It's hard to believe three little tugs can move that whopping great ship /

LEURA: Angel. Want a game of 'Listen'?

ANGEL: Don't start /

LEURA: Listen for all the screams of all the women murdered since time began. Including yours.

ANGEL: My only screams were screams of pleasure /

LEURA: You screamed so loudly you stopped the traffic on the bridge.

ANGEL: Bullcrap /

LEURA: No. You've forgotten. It's the shock. It takes years to wear off.

ANGEL: I'm going crazy.

LEURA: Angel ...

ANGEL: No. [*To* ROSE.] When I met Blue he promised to take me round the world.

LEURA: Angel /

ANGEL: After we got married we never left the fucking house. I should have known /

LEURA: Angel /

ANGEL: My mother used to say, 'Angel, peruse their shoes' /

LEURA: Want a game of 'Catch and Ravish'.

ANGEL: She said, 'What you can't tell from a man's footwear isn't worth knowing.'

ROSE: Really?

ANGEL: Two Tone — Cash Flow. Tan — Easy. Suede — Oral. First time I saw Blue he had on hand tooled, steel sprung, pointy toed, crocodile skin riding boots. Travelling shoes.

ROSE: You're lucky to have those memories of your mother, mine are all made up /

LEURA: Angel /

ANGEL: I said to Blue, 'My mother'd turn in her grave if she knew I was marrying a man with shoes like those.'

LEURA: What do you mean — she'd turn in her grave.

ANGEL: My mother O.D.'d in the ladies toilets at King's Cross station. Not that it's any of your business. [*Pause.*] O.D.. Opium overdose.

ROSE: Gosh.

LEURA: You're a motherless child ...

ANGEL: They've been closed to the public ever since.

ROSE: Gosh.

ANGEL: Yeah well. You play the percentages.

ROSE: Those toilets are a memorial to her Angel /

LEURA: Eve's a motherless child like us. I know it. We must try and warn her /

ANGEL: If she can't stand the burn she can get out of the saddle.

LEURA: She may discover us.

ANGEL: Sure. She's deaf. She's blind.

LEURA: She's alive.

ANGEL: God where's Blue.

LEURA: She's our only hope. If she were to discover us, the whole city would come. Blue would be destroyed. And the world would know our names.

ROSE: Three white tombstones ...

ANGEL: Crazy.

[EVE *enters.* ANGEL *starts to exit.*]

LEURA: Someone, somewhere, might shed a tear.

ANGEL: [*exits*] Blue!

ROSE: I hate to say this Leura but — you have become a monster.

[BLUE*'s Opera.*

BLUE *enters, a Prima Donna. He wears the ancient ice blue wedding dress. He carries an old wind up gramophone.*]

ANGEL: Sing to me.

ROSE: [*exiting*] I'm going to play 'Spook Roy'.

ANGEL: A love song.

LEURA: Rose!

[ROSE *stays.*]

BLUE: [*sings*] Oh, hit me kiss me kick me,
Crush me with your mouth,
Take me into heaven,
Take me north and south,
Take me round the world of you,
Leave me high and dry,
Prick me with your serpent's tongue,
Leave me here to die.
Oh, hit me kiss me kick me,
Bruise me with your eyes,
Shame me with the truth of you,
Choke me with your cries,
Take me round the world of you,
Leave me high and dry,
Lash me with your serpent's tail,
You're mightier than I,
Far mightier than I.

EVE: What an amazing dress.

BLUE: The fog's coming. Too soon.

EVE: Whose is it.

LEURA: Curiosity killed the cat.

ANGEL: Pussy's all gone.

ROSE: Remember when Blue drowned the kittens.

BLUE: My aching head.

EVE: Lie down.

ANGEL: Bed's where you do your best work.

BLUE: I hate the fog. Gives me writer's block. Do you like opera /

EVE: I don't really know much about it.

> [BLUE *puts on a crackly old opera record. He pretends to be listening to the music whenever he listens to the* GHOSTS.]

BLUE: Music sooths /

EVE: We have to talk.

BLUE: About what.

EVE: What's happening /

BLUE: It has nothing to do with you. Don't take it personally.

EVE: Well. It's hard not to. One minute we were making love /

ANGEL: [*about* EVE] I bet she's too stingy to have an orgasm.

BLUE: Leave it alone.

EVE: You've hardly said a word for days.

ANGEL: [*about* EVE] There's something very 'so what' about her tits.

ROSE: [*to* ANGEL] That's not true /

EVE: Blue. Please.

BLUE: 'Please'. A woman's word.

EVE: You can't even look at me.

ANGEL: Crow's feet already.

BLUE: I'm upset.

EVE: You're sorry it happened.

BLUE: Yes. And no. It was my wedding anniversary.

EVE: Right. So what happened the other night. It was because it was your wedding anniversary /

BLUE: Yes. No. It's not that simple.

ANGEL: Do you think she's prettier than me.

EVE: Look. I'm feeling really confused /

BLUE: [*to* EVE] I think you're one of the loveliest women I've ever met.

EVE: Thank you ...

ANGEL: He wasn't talking to you.

EVE: ... but you still wish it hadn't happened.

BLUE: Unlike you I can't take — bonking — lightly. When I *do* it, I lose myself, my Self. I'm overwhelmed. The past spurts forward into the present.

EVE: I see.

BLUE: No you don't.

EVE: Yes I do. This place is crawling with memories. You've never really told me anything about yourself. *Your* life. All your *wives*. [*Pause.*]

BLUE: Leura was an artist's model. I was still painting back in those days. She didn't approve of my paintings. She was a model, not a critic.

LEURA: Romanticism is a disease.

EVE: Was Rose a model too.

LEURA: A poet.

BLUE: Raised by the nuns. I wanted to be a poet but I wasn't any good at it. I minded that. [*Pause.*] She yearned to be gone from the first. Lasciatemi morir! Let me die — from morning till night.

EVE: How depressing /

BLUE: Catholicism has a lot to answer for. Angel — as I'm sure the Official Squirrel has told you — was a stripper. She wouldn't know how to spell the word 'work'.

ANGEL: F. U. C. K. U.
    [*Fog.*]

EVE: They all sound — exceptional /

BLUE: Yes.

LEURA: Fog.

BLUE: Although Leura tended to uniforms, being a suffragette. A mind of her own and no dress sense. Not like you girls today.

EVE: Ha ha.

ROSE: Foggy Macfog's here.

BLUE: Rosamund never changed her clothes. Forgetful. It wouldn't be an exaggeration to call her grubby. I had to wash everything by hand. Little white cotton garments.

ANGEL: L.U.V. that F.O.G..

BLUE: Angel, of course, was involved in an enterprise that required no clothes whatsoever. [*Pause.*] Insufferable.

ANGEL: Why are you doing this.

BLUE: Completely out of control, like this weather. I became lost in a labyrinth of her moods, her desires.

ANGEL: Liar.

BLUE: She accused me of being 'emotionally unavailable'. It was sheer self preservation.

EVE: I know what that feels like.

ANGEL: [*to* EVE] We fell madly in love with each other.

BLUE: But it's over now.

ANGEL: No.

BLUE: My *ex* wives.

ANGEL: No /

EVE: I've put up with my fair share of unpredictable behavior. It is like being lost in a labyrinth. Which is why I want to know where I stand /

BLUE: Come here.

ANGEL: Touch me.

BLUE: Listen. Listen. This is my favorite aria.

ANGEL: Touch me.

LEURA: No one will ever touch you again.

ANGEL: I'll go crazy if I'm not touched.

LEURA: What will send you mad is not being the favourite.

ANGEL: You should know.

LEURA: Not being desired.

ANGEL: He desires me as much as ever /

BLUE: Desire comes and goes, like the sea.

EVE: Is that what she's singing.

ANGEL: What the fuck is that supposed to mean.

EVE: Desire comes — and goes?

BLUE: Yes.

ANGEL: No.

LEURA: He has completed things with you.

ANGEL: No.

ROSE: Don't /

BLUE: Yes.

LEURA: You are betrayed.

ANGEL: You're just jealous.

LEURA: Me! Welcome jealousy. If you had the capacity to arouse me I would be your servant. But another century draws to its close and look at you. You diminish even the dead.

ANGEL: Get off your soap box /

LEURA: Invisible. Alone.

ANGEL: No /

LEURA: Untouchable /

ANGEL: Shut the fuck up /

LEURA: No one will ever touch you again. Ever.

ANGEL: [*quotes*] 'Nothing can cure me of my love for you Angel, unless death be the doctor!' He said.

LEURA: Unless death be the doctor.

   [*Silence.*]

ROSE: Oh Angel /

LEURA: Help us. Help us get through to her.

EVE: I'll leave you alone. With your memories.

BLUE: No. Memory should be a gentle mother. She should guide our steps. Give birth to conscience. But such sweet parenting has been denied us both. My memory is a monster. Her egg cracks open each day to reveal merely one more egg about to hatch.

ANGEL: I wish I could crack your skull open.

EVE: That's why I try to concentrate on the future.

BLUE: But what if dawn breaks at midnight, not dawn and each new day is born in darkness. When the black waves cradle the heavy white moon.

LEURA: Eve. The moon has fallen from the sky.

EVE: Blue /

BLUE: Listen.

LEURA: The moon has dropped out of the sky, the heavy white moon is the only flower on our grave. Worms, worms called fish, nibble the flesh from our bones.

BLUE: Yes.

LEURA: Buried deep under deep water.

ROSE: Blackrock, vile cathedral under the waves. Wrecked ships in the vestry, your hair gets caught on them /

ANGEL: I have to feel my body. I have to. My skin.

ROSE: Soft white arms, like doves. Beautiful Angel.

BLUE: Beautiful.

ANGEL: I *will* go mad.

BLUE: Mad.

LEURA: I'd be old. My hair would be white as snow.

BLUE: Her beautiful hair, crimson as blood.

LEURA: The early morning sun a torch to my papery hands. I would burn.

ROSE: The warm midday sun.

LEURA: I would burn.

ANGEL: The black frozen sun.

LEURA: Death to the Winter King. Spring.

ROSE: Spring. Death.

BLUE: Death.

ANGEL: Death. Love.

BLUE: Love.

ANGEL: Stark fucking raving /

ROSE: Lasciatemi morir.

BLUE: God I love opera.

[*Pause.*]

EVE: It's not in English.

[*Much fog.*]

BLUE: [*referring to wedding dress*] Put it on.

EVE: What did you have in mind.

BLUE: For me.

ROSE: Eve. Turn off the music.

ANGEL: My dress.

EVE: You're feverish /

BLUE: No.

EVE: What are you doing.

ANGEL: My dress.

BLUE: It's yours.

ROSE: Turn off the music.

EVE: I don't want to.

LEURA: Oh pretty dress. The colour of cyanide.

ROSE: Turn off the music.

LEURA: Blue moon.

ANGEL: L'amour blue. Blue movies.

LEURA: Blue murder /

EVE: Blue. Don't /

BLUE: Blue. The perfect colour.

ROSE: The music /

BLUE: When the devil finally takes her, Eve will collect his red eczema and use it as rouge. Then her blue lips and breasts will glow like fire opals and her petticoats crackle with electricity.

ROSE: Turn off the music.

[EVE *turns off the music.*]

ROSE: She heard.

EVE: Opera obviously gives you a real hard on but it doesn't have quite the same effect on me.

ROSE: She heard.

LEURA: She's got to see us. We'll play 'Killed Off'.

EVE: I'm sick to death of games. You don't need a 'personal assistant'. Basically you were after a /

BLUE: A what.

EVE: You were advertising for a mistress.

BLUE: No.

EVE: Fine. I give up. Enough's enough /

BLUE: What's mine is yours Eve. If you want it. [*Exits.*] Marry me.

SCENE TWO

Courtyard.
They play 'Jump the Broom'.

LEURA: Quick! 'Killed Off'!

ROSE: Eve! Watch this!

LEURA: Carmen!

ROSE: Stabbed!

LEURA: Ophelia!

ROSE: Drowned!

LEURA: Lucia!

ROSE: Crackers!

LEURA: Isolde!

ROSE: Ravished! Tosca!

LEURA: Flew! Mimi!

ROSE: Froze! Butterfly!

ANGEL: [*at* EVE] Stabbed!
    [*Pause.*]

LEURA: Thank you. Tess!

ANGEL: Bugger! I don't know Tess /

ROSE: Annie Karenini!

LEURA: Squashed! Clytemnestra!

ANGEL: Death by death! Scarlet!

LEURA: Who.

ANGEL: Scarlet. She lost her true love. Her child. Everything /

LEURA: Camille!

ROSE: Consumed!

ANGEL: It's my go! Consumption! Films! Marilyn! [*Pause.*] Tricked!

LEURA: Lavinia!

ROSE: No, no. I know it, wait /

LEURA: Chopped! Zenobia!

EVE: Hello?

ANGEL: [*at* EVE] Eve!

LEURA: Married!

EVE: Hello? Is somebody here. Who are you.

ROSE: Leura ...

EVE: What's happening to me. What's happening to me. Who's there.
    [LYLE *appears out of the fog.*]

EVE: Lyle.

ROSE: A boy /

ANGEL: What's going on /

LEURA: Be quiet.

EVE: Lyle ...

LYLE: Are you alright.

EVE: What are you doing here.

LYLE: I've been worried sick. Why haven't you called me?

EVE: I don't know.

LYLE: What's happened to you.

EVE: Why are you looking at me like that.

LYLE: You're white as a sheet.

EVE: Stop it.

LYLE: Your eyes ...

EVE: Stop looking at me like that /

LYLE: Your eyes /

EVE: What are you talking about /

LYLE: What's going on /

EVE: Nothing. [*Pause.*] How long have I been here?

LYLE: What are *you* talking about.

EVE: It doesn't make sense /

LYLE: When I didn't hear from you I thought — out with the old in with the new /

EVE: How long have I been here /

LYLE: This has gone far enough. We're gone.

WIVES: No.

EVE: No.

LYLE: We're out of here. Now.

ROSE: The Witch's call from *Counting Cats and Cauldrons*.

LYLE: Evelyn /

ROSE: Quick!

EVE: It doesn't make sense.

ROSE: Bid bid bid! Come on!

LYLE: Look at me.

WIVES: Bid bid bid!

LYLE: It's alright /

EVE: No /

WIVES: Come bid, come bid, come bid /

LYLE: It's alright /

WIVES: Come suck, come suck, come suck!

EVE: Hear that.

LYLE: What.

WIVES: Come bid come bid come bid!

EVE: Listen.

WIVES: Come suck come suck come suck!

EVE: Listen.

ROSE: One two three.

LYLE: Evelyn.

WIVES: Eve!

LYLE: Evelyn.

WIVES: Eve!

EVE: One pure note.

LYLE: You're not making any bloody sense.

EVE: Eve ...

LYLE: Where is he. I want to talk to him.

EVE: I'm not leaving.

LYLE: You're coming with me. Evelyn /

EVE: Evelyn. Dust. [*Pause.*] I'm not going back. You don't understand. When my mother left she used up my future to do it. My share of luck. Sold me to the devil. I'm not going back. I won't have a predictable life.

LYLE: A predictable life. Great. It's him isn't it /

EVE: No. It's not Blue. It's not the job. It's this place. I feel as if there's a rope here, tugging at me.

LYLE: There's something you're not telling me.

EVE: There's nothing. [*Pause.*] He's asked me to marry him.

LYLE: You can't be serious. You don't even know what day it is /

EVE: I was dreaming. I'm awake now /

LYLE: Are you in love with him.

EVE: I don't know.

LYLE: How can you not know.

EVE: It's not that /

LYLE: Have you been sleeping with him.

EVE: No. Once.

LYLE: Oh that's alright then /

EVE: It's not that. Try to understand. This isn't — personal /

LYLE: What are you saying! What are you. A machine? I'm a person. You're a person. I assume he's a fucking person /

EVE: No! No — it's not about that. It's got nothing to do with you or me or our feelings /

LYLE: I don't believe this.

EVE: How many chances do we get to change our lives.

LYLE: Thousands ...

EVE: One.

LYLE: ... I feel sick.

ROSE: Oh the poor things /

ANGEL/LEURA: Shhh!

EVE: One and you have to keep taking it /

LYLE: You *are* in love. Say it. Say it. [*Pause.*] We've known each other too long for me to tell you what I think of you right now. [*Exits.*]

EVE: Lylo ...

ROSE: Lylo. It's so unfair /

ANGEL: Eve!

EVE: Alright. [*Pause.*] Come on then. Who are you. [*Pause.*] Come on then. Who are you.
  [GHOSTS' *Aria.*]

LEURA: Eve. The smell of a bloody knife. It stinks.

ROSE: Leura!

ANGEL: [*about* LEURA] What's she doing.

LEURA: Terrible. Strong. All the hot blood, scattered like petals.

ROSE: No.

LEURA: Rose. Rose. That was her name.

ROSE: You mustn't /

LEURA: We must. All three. Before the fog lifts. [*Pause.*] I hadn't smelt anything in fifty years, it nearly took the top of my head off. The heat made her skirt fly right up around her waist. The furnace of blood lifted her, she paddled and paddled her thin arms and then she hit the ceiling.
  [ROSE *flies heavenward.*]

ROSE: Sweet Mother of God.

LEURA: She looked so surprised.

ANGEL: What's happening /

ROSE: Blue held the small blood in his hands /

LEURA: Angel the same. Laughing then shouting then dead /

ROSE: Run Angel, run! Your beautiful red disappears like smoking oil into his infinite blue which swallows even the stars. The sky, black, black /

ANGEL: He showed me his knife /

LEURA: I ran my hands along it. It felt warm. A temperature all its own.

ANGEL: I held it /

LEURA: a shiver along the blade as I handled it. Blue stiffened /

ANGEL: our eyes met —

LEURA: three bones snapped inside my wrist /

ANGEL: he came for me /

LEURA: the knife opened Blue's hand /

ANGEL: he came for me /

LEURA: I got in first /

ROSE: he took my life /

LEURA: I took my life /

ROSE: my child's life /

LEURA: my child's life /

ANGEL: the blade /

LEURA: a freezing blast /

ANGEL: filled me full /

LEURA: knocked me flat /

ANGEL: I fell /

LEURA: a great silence holding me under /

ANGEL: I couldn't breathe /

LEURA: Blue's eyes so wide creeping over to where I lay /

ANGEL: bent over me /

LEURA: watching in wonder /

ANGEL: like a new father bent over me /

LEURA: retrieved the knife and then, such a blood my ears filled with the roar of it /

ROSE: roses /

LEURA: dark bloody spurts /

ANGEL: his eyes /

43

ROSE: in the distance /

LEURA: his hair drenched /

ROSE: a storm of petals /

ANGEL: his eyes /

LEURA: his beard a sop to it as he leaned close /

EVE: Blood.

LEURA: closer /

ANGEL: filled with — hate.

LEURA: His beard a blue sop as he leaned closer to see what should never be seen.

EVE: Not real.

LEURA: Yes. Real.

EVE: Not. Real.

LEURA: Murder has married us to our husband.

EVE: The Nowhere Stairs. The Sydney Harbour Bridge.

LEURA: [*quiet, close*] Not real.

[*Silence.*]

Death is strong. But you're alive. Life is stronger than death.

ACT FIVE

SCENE ONE

Blackrock.
ROY*'s broom is decorated with white ribbons. The* GHOSTS *enter.*

ROY: Here I am, Sweeper, son of a sweeper and son of Blackrock,
the mother I love best. Spring was here a long time ago. Light.
Sun and moss, green and velvet even on the flat rocks. We were
never submerged, only at Sickle Tide. Wavelets. Wavelets then.
The tide takes memory and sometimes delivers it, I rolled in my
mother's lap, Blackrock was my cradle on the waves. Birds came.
They made a mess. And nests. There are no birds now. Blue is a
winter king. The tides are unpredictable. Fog. Wheeling back
and forward and back across the harbour. Shadows, too, too many,
like in a wrecked ship at the bottom, it doesn't make sense. It's
not for me to understand. I sweep. Today is the wedding feast,
the opera table set with black wine and figs. At dawn the moon
went behind a cloud. I was Eve's only bridesmaid. I helped her
put on the wedding dress. It rained, the rain swept away the fog
with wide sweeps, vertically. Next a sequence of fierce random
sweeps, straight up and down. We stood on the Nowhere stairs
in the rain, the morning was fair enough in its own shades. I
performed the ceremony, which is a part of my official duties.
Being Sweeper I know the rhythms. I only forgot them once
when Rosamund was the bride. I didn't forget them today. They
were all pronounced. 'These two, calleth the Corascene bitch
and the Armenian dogge — being put together in the alchemical
vessel of the sepulcher, do bite one another cruelly, and by their
great poyson, and furious rage, they never leave one another,
from the moment they have seized on one another, till both by
their slavering venom and mortall hurts, be all of a goareblood,
over all the parts of their bodies and finally, killing one another,

be stewed in their proper venome, which after their death, changeth them into living and permanent water, before which time they lose in their corruption and putrefaction, first their natural formes, to take afterwards only one new, more noble form. Thus is holy marriage.' Eve says, 'I will.' I say, 'It is true without lie, certain and most veritable, that what is below is like what is above and that what is above is like what is below, to perpetrate the miracle of one thing.' Blue pronounces, 'Solve et coagula.' [*Pause.*] An unusual thing happened. Gusts, with a swirling movement, clockwise! Snatched all of Eve's long veils, they were raised up like sails in the sky, I was speechless. Then they fell into the harbour. Events like that pass too quickly. Eve's hair streamed down, Blue said never mind, a woman is her own veil — something like that, meaning her hair. And another thing. At dawn, when I wrapped Eve's sashes, I tidied my hands over her stomach, I could feel her pulses. They're very strong. All of a sudden I remembered when we were green. You could lie around then, roll around and sometimes the moss gave me a rash. Spring. We'll see.

[ROY *carefully puts down his broom.*]

SCENE TWO

BLUE *carries* EVE *over the threshold.* ROY *throws confetti.*

BLUE: Sweep it up later Roy.
    [EVE *throws her bouquet to* ROY. *He catches it and exits.*]
EVE: Don't put me down. I feel so ... excited. And strange. I wish you could keep carrying me over the threshold. Forever.
BLUE: Forever. Your wish is my command.
    [*Carries her across again.*]
EVE: What a night. I've never seen a moon like it. I didn't know what it was when it first broke the horizon, it was so huge. And the water. Standing on end like silver fur. [*Pause.*] I love you. I have from the first day.
    [*They kiss.*]

46

ROSE: The moon will pull the water right off the edge of the world tonight.

BLUE: You make me happy, it seems like my first time. What's mine is yours.

EVE: I'm dizzy with it. Drunk on moonlight.

BLUE: You need some wine. But first.

[BLUE *produces the Alphabet Knife.*]

For you.

EVE: It's beautiful.

[EVE *accepts the knife.*]

There's something engraved here ...

BLUE: Your A B C's.

EVE: An Alphabet Knife.

BLUE: Extremely rare.

EVE: Extremely sharp.

BLUE: Extremely convincing.

[*Silence.*]

EVE: Thank you.

[EVE *lays the knife between them and raises a toast.*]

The future.

BLUE: To marriage.

EVE: To life. [*Pause.*] This is such a magic place.

BLUE: Your home. [*Pause.*] Eve dances on a table surrounded by the glittering throng. [*He undresses her.*] While the devil stands by holding her shoes.

EVE: A girl should keep both feet firmly on the ground when she's dancing with the devil. Let me keep it on a while longer. I'll never wear it again.

BLUE: Hitch it up.

EVE: Wait. [*Pause.*] Wait. Erotic tradition. Put things off for as long as possible.

BLUE: Good girl.

Very long pause.

EVE: I'm pregnant.

BLUE: Too soon.

EVE: I'm full to bursting. With your dead women. We are married.

All of us. You use me. All of you. Angel. Leura. Rosemary. You'd turn me into your nest like a bunch of horrible old magpies /

ROSE: No!

LEURA: Pick up the knife.

ANGEL: Cut out his heart.

LEURA: One pair of hands, easier than baking a cake.

BLUE: My curse. To love what would destroy me /

LEURA: To love what would destroy you. Always the romantic.

BLUE: Romanticism's my favorite toy.

LEURA: Romanticism is a disease.

BLUE: Romanticism is a beautiful woman with a nasty surprise hidden under her skirts.

ANGEL: Words. Filthy words /

BLUE: Words? Yes. I'm my father's son. My father made words flutter like moths around the candles he burned to read them by.

LEURA: Your father died the night you were born.

BLUE: My father kept a copy of the Old Testament by his right hand just so he could listen to the rumble of vowels turning between the pages /

LEURA: One look at you and he died.

EVE: Why? Why is this happening?

BLUE: My father painted his lovers — to illustrate my A B C's but what pictures —

LEURA: What happened to your mother.

BLUE: My mother. A succubus dressed as a madonna smiling across my nursery. The Mona Lisa.

ANGEL: Stop using words /

BLUE: My father gave birth to me. On the banks of the Pactolus in Lydia. Dionysus arrived, uninvited, the bad fairy at my christening /

EVE: No more stories /

BLUE: My father gave birth to me. At the Globe and wrapped me up in Prospero's cloak. It was dusty. I sneezed. The actors laughed/

EVE: No more stories.

BLUE: I love my father.

LEURA: He would have hated you.

BLUE: He gave me history for my playground /

LEURA: Your version of history is a lie. The emperor's new clothes.

EVE: Stop it.

BLUE: My favorite story. The naked emperor will always point at the trussed up crowd and have the last laugh /

LEURA: No. Only the dead hold history — in their mouths. The living must lie.

EVE: Stop! [*Pause.*] Why are they dead. The truth.

    Pause.

BLUE: Sweet Mother Nature and her pretty daughters.

LEURA: Pick up the knife /

BLUE: Your mother hasn't abandoned you, Evie, you are her incubator, she breeds in you. Your body is her clock that never needs winding. Month in month out. The blood. The suck. The fetid wallow that was our prison before my father gave birth to language.

LEURA: Pick up the knife /

BLUE: My poor old dad turns himself to marble, his glorious arm raised in homage to beauty, to art and your mother eats that marble like leprosy through flesh. Accept your fate. I create, you destroy. Your true nature? In the swaddling of your thighs poetry is diminished and falls silent. Always and forever. Again and again. What my father's family creates your mother's family destroys and history is merely the record of their bloody feud.

LEURA: Liar!

BLUE: [*about* LEURA] Behold. The Past. While I painted her free she lay helpless in my bed. Clutching a hot water bottle to her swollen belly. Breeding. Breeding the future which would destroy me. Always and forever. Again and again.

ROSE: Evie, look at me. Look at me /

BLUE: [*about* ROSE] Innocence. A flower always about to bloom. Preserved in death. Perfected in death. Never dust. Always and forever.

ANGEL: You are a monster.

BLUE: I'm an artist.

ANGEL: Sure. Violent kid's cartoons /

BLUE: What people want. [*About* ANGEL.] The Mystery. Dance of the seven veils. Nakedness unsolved. A naked woman is man's waking dream. Of death. Always and forever.

ANGEL: Unnatural.

BLUE: No. Nature is unnatural! A litany of death and destruction.

ROSE: Evie, look at me.

BLUE: But an artist can squeeze a drop of beauty even out of death. Is it unnatural for me to press a grape and make wine. I don't think so.

ROSE: Look at me.

    Pause.

EVE: They should have been a dream of life, not death.

BLUE: [*about* EVE] The Future. Heroic woman. Blind. Deaf. On the run. Indiscriminate mother nature now brandishes a sword. You'd destroy everything man has created and not even stop to mourn. You are pregnant. With the end of the world. My curse to love you.

ROSE: No. You *are* pregnant. You're carrying the spring.

LEURA: Choose.

EVE: If I use that knife I'll be like you. If I don't I'll be like you. One or the other. Why.

ANGEL: Life or death.

LEURA: Choose.

EVE: You say you're transforming nature into art but I look at your dead women and I don't see art. Oh — they are transformed. From life to death. Murdered. Since when has killing women been called art. [*Pause.*] You say we have to destroy each other because you're a man and I'm a woman. But there is someone who loves me, a young man who wants life for me as much as he wants it for himself. You *are* a liar. The truth isn't some stupid old feud. You're scared. Of your own fate. You use up young life — life that's full of hope — to preserve your bloody history. You want to control birth. Death. Even the weather. No wonder you can't stop telling stories. How many stories does it take, how many paintings, how many dead women will it take to keep your bloody fate from reaching Blackrock and ravishing you. My future for your past? Never. [*Pause.*] Here's my life line. It's long. I'm young. I will live. Even they are more alive that you are.

[*The* GHOSTS *regain their sense of smell.*]

EVE: Rosemary Allen. Angel Brokowski. Leura Mackenzie. Help me now and I'll never forget you.

LEURA: What's happening /

ROSE: Leura. What is it /

ANGEL: The ocean. I can smell the ocean /

LEURA: But we can't /

ROSE: Angel's right. Oh /

LEURA: It is /

ROSE: yes /

[*The* GHOSTS *feel their own bodies.*]

ANGEL: My hands. My hands. Leura. Don't be frightened /

LEURA: I can't move /

[ANGEL *touches* ROSE. ROSE *screams.*]

BLUE: They merely grow stronger to welcome you.

[BLUE *and* EVE *both move to the knife.*]

ANGEL: No. Leura!

[LEURA *puts out her hand.* BLUE *walks into it and recoils.*]

BLUE: A fine game. Very fine.

EVE: No more games.

ROSE: Blue! [*Dies.*] Lasciatemi morir!

[*The* GHOSTS *rush between* BLUE *and* EVE. *In a celebration of resurrecting* GHOSTS, *the* GHOSTS *die, they get up.*]

ANGEL: Again.

LEURA: Die.

ROSE: Again! Again!

LEURA: Always and forever.

ROSE: Lasciatemi morir! [*Gets up.*] The floor, so close, I'm cross eyed /

LEURA: [*dies*] Oh my heavens. It is close.

ROSE: [*dies*] Lasciatemi morir! [*Gets up, dies.*] Lasciatemi morir! [*Gets up.*] Oh the floor. The beautiful floor.

ANGEL: Die. Always and forever /

ROSE: Look out!

ANGEL: Boo.

BLUE: [*to* ANGEL] Don't touch me. Monster /

LEURA: Live. Again and again /

ROSE: [*to* LEURA] Your hair, your beautiful hair. Rosemary Rosemary Rosemary. My hand. Your hands your hands oh Leura your hands Angel. Beautiful Angel, soft ...

> [EVE *gets to the knife. A blast of spring.*]

ROSE: Oh.

LEURA: Green. I smell green /

> [ROSE *speaks in tongues.*]

ROSE: [*overlapping*] Yramesor Yramesor Legna Aruel Aruel

BLUE: That knife is forged in a blue fire /

ROSE: [*overlapping*] Legna Yramesor Aruel

BLUE: it sings of a world with no end /

ROSE: [*overlapping*] Legna Yramesor Aruel Legna Aruel

BLUE: how beautiful is that song

ROSE: [*overlapping*] Legna Yramesor Aruel Yramesor. Eve.

BLUE: Always accompanied by a woman.

ROY: [*offstage sings*] A flock of stars a tree of leaves a bird's nest
made of sand,

BLUE: Roy!

ROY: [*offstage sings*] a bush of birds a crown of leaves a blue egg
in the hand,

BLUE: Roy!

ROY: [*offstage sings*] a parrot fish from right to left across the sky so
blue,

A swallow flies out of the moon I know my
love is true.

LEURA: Gone.

ANGEL: He's waiting for the fucking birds to come back /

ROSE: Blackrock green

LEURA: Spring

ROSE: Soft as velvet

LEURA: Spring

ANGEL: Death

ROSE: Love

LEURA: Life

>   [*Silence.*]

BLUE: An Alphabet Knife can never be turned against its maker.

EVE: You gave it to me. I accept it. Thank you.

>   [EVE *sacrifices* BLUE.]

BLUE: [*dies*] Good girl.

>   [*The* GHOSTS *and* BLUE *disappear.*]

ROY: [*offstage sings*] A flock of stars a tree of leaves a bird's nest made of sand,

>   A bush of birds a crown of leaves a blue egg in the hand,
>
>   A parrot fish from right to left across the sky so blue,
>
>   A swallow flies out of the moon I know my love is true.
>
>   A song of spring a crown of leaves I know my love is true.

SCENE THREE

Courtyard.
EVE *throws the bloody knife into the sea.*
Silence.

EVE: Roy. Roy. Quickly. There. See that ...

>   *Pause.*

ROY: Bodies.

EVE: [*relieved*] Yes. Yes /

ROY: Their hair's all tangled up together. Their arms are wrapped around each other. Three /

EVE: What colour is their hair /

ROY: I can't tell. This sunrise — it's making the waves bright red /

EVE: Not the sun. The whole harbour is red. The red sea casts its shadow on the yellow sun. [*Pause.*] Look!

ROY: Seagulls!

EVE: Women.

ROY: Sweeping the ocean /

EVE: Women /

ROY: one thousand /

EVE: being carried by the current to the shore.

    [Cry of a thousand seagulls. Red dawn into light.]

THE END